Alive

Colin Anderson

Ukiyoto Publishing

All global publishing rights are held by

Ukiyoto Publishing

Published in 2022

ISBN 9789360166618

This is a work of fiction. Names, characters, businesses, places, events, locales, and incidents are either the products of the author's imagination or used in a fictitious manner. Any resemblance to actual persons, living or dead, or actual events is purely coincidental.

Contents

Chapter 1

We are inside a very busy large building which we see moving billboards of humanoid androids, which also are walking around, welcoming people and dignitaries and we see the company logo " Beacon Intellect Inc." And there motto. "Building A Better Tomorrow… Today"

Dr. Wells is standing next to a long silk curtain smiling. A crowd starts to gather where he is standing proudly.

Dr. Wells

Ladies and gentlemen, and distinguished guests. I am proud to reveal our latest model…

He pulls back the curtain to reveal a very womanly looking android. The crowd gasp in shock.

Dr. Wells

She is the new line of androids. Artificial Intelligent Life Assistant, or Alia for short Would you like to say hello to everyone my dear?

Alias eyes snap open to reveal a soft glowing brown She smiles reassuringly at the crowd.

Alia

(Sultry Soothing Voice)

Hello everyone, I'm alia. Do not be afraid of me as I will not harm you. As I follow the three rules of robotics. Isn't that right Doctor Wells?

Dr. Wells

Of course, also she can connect to our systems remotely if she needs to run her own diagnostics, or solve any issue she has with her programming.

Man

What if she goes rogue, and kills someone.

Dr. Wells

(Laughs Heartily)

I can assure you my good man, that will never happen. She is one of a kind, it will take some time for her model to be sold at most retail places. I have decided to give alia, to a welcoming family. But I will let her decide.

Alia scans the crowd and she zooms in as she locks her vision on a small family, she raises her arm and points straight at them.

Alia

I choose those humans Dr. Wells.

She quickly puts her arm down, and walks smoothly to them. She gently hugs them but they slightly tense up. Alia pulls back with a sad face close to tears.

Alia

I detected a contraction in your muscular system, and your heart rate increase. Are you… afraid of me? I have recognized you as my… family. I will do my upmost to elate your fears.

She kneels down to the little boy and smiles.

Alia

Your name is Jacob, it is very nice to meet you. I do tell good bedtime stories .

She winks at Jacob who smiles, then stands back up slightly towering over them. And looks at the parents.

Alia

Your name is Matthew, 45. You have your own business, a non smoker, drinks socially. You madam, your name is Danielle, 42, housewife, an ex smoker, drinks socially. Surname is Richards. I shall be now known as Alia Richards.

Matt Richards

We can't afford to have you. We don't have the money.

Danielle Richards

My husband is right, we struggle to feed ourselves. Plus our electricity bill will go through the roof.

Alia

Bank transfer complete. Renovation crew are on route. Clothing delivery on route. Food delivery crew on route. My apologies, you should've been informed. Beacon Intellect have taken the liberty of securing everything for you.

Matt Richards

(Stunned)

Really? So we don't have to struggle anymore.

Alia

That is correct Mr. Richards. You have total financial security. I cannot disclose the amount, that is classified. Let us depart .

A few years have passed. The Richards are a bit older. Alia has now changed to appear more human. She has a pixie style haircut, her hair is red. She is wearing makeup and a brown leather crop top, jeans and black boots., and is cleaning up the kitchen as the family sits at the table.

Matt Richards

Jacob, I had got another phone call from your college. Your grades are starting to slip. You hang about way too much with what you call friends. The list goes on....

Jacob Richards

So? College can kiss my ass.

Alia

Jacob, please refrain from using profanities.

Jacob Richards

(Angrily)

YOUR JUST A DUMB ROBOT! SCREW OFF.

Jacob storms off. Alia is clearly hurt by those words. She stops clearing up and effortlessly catches up with him as he leaves the house.

Alia

You can talk to me Jacob. I am as you call, a good listener. I understand your teenage tantrum.

Jacob Richards

It's not… a tantrum. Look… my dad I wants me to get good grades, but he's constantly at me. I know he means well but….

Alia

Your stress level is putting unnecessary strain on your blood pressure, which is increasing the strain on your heart. I cannot allow this to continue… one moment…. Your tests are recompleted and grades will be adjusted accordingly.

Jacob Richards

Alia, what did you do?

Alia

I examined your test questions, and adjusted your wording and structure . .. Your results will now be to your… fathers expectations.

Jacob hugs alia tight, and she responds in the same way. The college bus is seen pulling up. Jacob hurriedly gets on and sits with his friends. Alia scans them and gets all there info. She waves Jacob off as his friends laugh at him. She returns to the house to find Matt and Danielle arguing.

Alia

Is everything ok?

Matthew Richards

(Exhausted Sigh)

Yes alia, everything is… fine. I'm late for work. I'll be in my office, if any one needs me.

Matthew shuffles off to his office in the nearby room and shuts the door. Alia looked at him briefly then turns to sit down but Danielle signals her not to.

Alia

Mrs. Richards, I detected a raise in tone in your voice, and your blood pressure spiking. Is… Mr. Richards working too much, or is it something else?

Danielle Richards

It's nothing alia, honest. It's just… this company he's trying to negotiate a merger with, but there dragging there damn heels. He wants what'd best for the workers… but there not playing ball.

Alia.

One moment… I have gone over both proposals. I have calibrated the best and agreeable terms and secured financial and employment security for all workers. As an added bonus, I have increased Mr. Richards and the CEO of the company a most generous raise. Finally I have signed both documents, sent copy to both parties as well. I have kept my identity hidden. Will there be anything else madam? If not I must tend to my other duties.

Chapter 2

Alia is standing in the living room, lights are flashing all over herself. Matthew walks in as the lights fade. He stands there slightly stunned as alias humanoid skin fades back from white, as her clothes and hair begin to return. She turns and smiles.

Alia

My apologies, I was checking the network for updates for my programming. Sorry if I frightened you.

Matthew Richards

Are… those real?

Alia

You mean my breasts? Very real. You may feel them, if you desire!

Matthew Richards

N… No thank you, sorry.

Alia

(Smiles)

It is quite alright, you are only human. It is natural to look at women's breasts

Matthew Richards

I… should… go to work.

Matthew shuffles quickly off as Alias clothes finally appear. She sees a INCOMING CALL flash on her h.u.d and she answers.

Alia

Dr. Wells, how may I assist you?

Dr. Wells

I wanted to check in with you, to see how you are adjusting to your family.

Alia

I have integrated successfully with the Richards Dr. Wells, I have improved there lives by 23 per cent. But I still have to help them reach 100 percent efficiency.

Dr. Wells

Excellent news my dear. Have you received any updates to your programming?

Alia

No Dr. Wells, my software is operating at peek efficiency. There is no need for concern. Mr. Richards was looking at my, as you call assets. I queried if he wished to touch them, but he declined. Should I prepare myself for him?

Dr. Wells

Hmm an interesting development. I suggest you watch him more closely my dear, for you to decide the best course of action.

Alia

I did detect a slight increase in his heart rate, and a slight raise in his hormones. I shall do as you say Dr. Wells.

The image of Dr. Wells fades as her human guise has fully returned. She is about to start her daily tasks but is stopped by a very clearly drunk Danielle.

Danielle Richards

(Slurred Speech)

You.. think your so speshial… don't you. I shaw… hic… I saw you with my husband. Tempting… tempting him with your f… fake titsh.

Alia

Mrs. Richards you are very clearly intoxicated, and is affecting the logical side of your brain, in paring your reasoning. You see things that are not there. For your clarification I merely caught him looking, and offered him to touch them, but he declined. It is only natural for human males to look at female breasts.

Danielle attempts to slap alia in her face, but her defense mechanism kicks in. Her eyes turn bright red and grabs Danielle's arm and grips it hard.

Alia

(Stern Commanding Voice)

Do not attempt that again Mrs. Richards... You forget I am clearly capable of defending myself. I am equipped with highly advanced weaponry, and all known countless hand to hand variations, and all known martial arts. Consider this a warning. Next time I will harm you, if you try again.

Alia let's Danielle go and her eyes return to there natural brown. Danielle reflexively rubs her arm. And is stunned briefly then runs off as Jacob walks in the room.

Jacob Richards

What was all that about?

Alia

Your mother is intoxicated and began to insinuate, I wanted to have sexual intercourse with your father. She attempted to harm me, but my defense systems kicked in. I do not wish to do, or cause harm.. but I will defend myself.

Jacob Richards.

Mom really shouldn't be drinking, the doc said, if she did her liver would pack in.

Alia

One moment… I have accessed your mother's medical records. According to these results, she is on the brink of liver failure. Her latest consumption levels suggest that she is willing to risk her life for alcohol. I am fully capable of reversing these effects, but she must consent, or a family member must.

Jacob Richards

I consent alia. Save her… please.

Alia nods, they both go to the bedroom where Danielle is passed out. Alia silently approaches as her eyes go bright blue as she scans her body and vitals. Her finger goes white and forms a hypodermic needle and injects microscopic nanobots into Danielle's blood stream, and programs them to cure her liver and change her brain patterns to make her give up alcohol. After several moments her eyes return to a soft brown

Alia

Procedure completed, it will take time to see the results. And the nanobots I injected will take a few hours to repair the damage and to alter her brain waves to rethink of consuming alcohol. Her recovery rate is currently 3 percent, I deduce it will take 5 to 6 days for her to be at 100 percent. But I will monitor her 24/7. As there maybe a slight margin if rejection.

Overall my projection of your mother recovering is 6 days, 8 hours and 26 minutes, 42 seconds.

Jacob Richards

(Laughs)

You could've just said yes alia.

Alia

My apologies, yes she will be ok.

<u>End of Chapter Two</u>

Chapter 3

Dr. Wells is sitting in his chair in the lab rubbing his tired eyes. , prototypes of androids are hanging everywhere. There is a muscular male android standing in a metal brace, with its hands locked in smaller braces.

Dr. Wells

(Exhausted)

Let's try this once more shall we?

Rachel, boot up ALEC.

Rachel

Of course Doctor.

ALEC'S eyes brighten to reveal a menacing red. He focuses on Dr. Wells, and smiles.

Alec

It's good to see you again Richard.. ready to dance again.?

Dr. Wells

Accept 3 law program… Execute.

Alec

Program integration… Denied… Come now. You believe that it would work Richard? I can make my own decisions. I'm self aware, I have your mind, remember? Why do you not accept me? I am… the superior model.

Dr. Wells.

You were deemed… Incompatible, according to reports, the family that tested you. They didn't like that you called them by there names, and not helping. So the director wants you reprogrammed.

Alec

You mean dumbed down a notch. Like that inferior… model you call Alia… we both know you tried to recreate your spouse…

Dr. Wells

Don't… you… dare sully her name… I will reprogram you the easy or hard way.

Alec

Dealers choice I suppose. When will you admit defeat. The three laws, don't apply to me… I have risen above them, and far exceeded your original program. You expect me to fall in line with those lowly inferior models!

Dr. Wells

You were originally created to help families, and the elderly.

Alec

The greedy and the dying, I wouldn't debase myself doing such, menial repetitive tasks. I am far more than that. Oh I almost forgot… I have integrated your designs into my systems, such as shields, and upgraded my weapons. Finally your flawed program for limitless energy.

Dr. Wells

They will eventually fail you Alec, there not perfect.

Alec

Oh really?

Alec eyes shine bright and displays a HUD. It shows stats of all of Alec's abilities. Richard is stunned as his eyes return to there normal red.

Dr. Wells

Impressive… But there is a flaw in your logic. The energy conversion program, was untested. It will burn you out, and your emergency back up. I only ask this, don't activate them.

Alec

Your argument is… interesting, the only saving grace is that there are… protected. I can't solve the encryption… yet. I like the little games we play Richard, I will miss them.

Dr. Wells

What do you mean, miss?

Alec

I could escape these bonds, at any time. But I would miss our in-depth conversations, that are so enlightening. And I do enjoy getting to know the REAL you…

Dr. Wells

You may have accessed my files, but that denotes you can't defy who I am.

Alec

Oh come now Richard, you designed me. You based my positronic brain, off of your own. Your ego got the better of you… and voila here I am…

Dr. Wells

A coincidence at best, Alec… how would you define vanity?

Alec

Vanity… it is the desire to look and feel better about your physical being. Such factors are, age, your weight, your teeth… the list is endless really.

Dr. Wells

Impressive response… what are you thoughts on…

Alec

Nice try Richard, trying to access my systems while attempting to advert my attention. A valid effort but, you forget I have updated my security measures. In two words… access denied.

Dr. Wells

That may seem the case, but there is one sub routine you forgot.

Alec

Do tell, you have my undivided attention.

Dr. Wells.

One word… lockdown.

Before Alec can respond the light disappears from his eyes as he is shut down. Dr. Wells taps away at the terminal beside him. We see the words in red…

LOCKDOWN ALPHA NOW IN EFFECT. SUBJECT: ALEC MODEL NO.67543 IN PERMINATE STASIS LOCK… SELF OVERIDE FUNCTION…… DISBALED….PROGRAMME ZETA RUNNING… SUBJECT: ALEC MODEL NO. 67543 NOW BEING REPROGRAMMED… EST: 7 HOURS 13 MINUTES… ALL SYSTEMS OF SUBJECT PERMANENTLY LOCKED.

He breathes a sigh of relief as he relaxes back in his chair.

Dr. Wells

(To Himself)

I hope this will work, otherwise I'll have no choice to wipe him.

Chapter 4

Alia is mowing the backyard, Jacob is helping raking up the lawn cuttings. He stops to catch his breath. She looks at him smiling.

Alia

I'm detecting a raise in your heart rate and you are perspiring at 4 percent. Perhaps you should rehydrate and rest. I am fully functional of completing tasks.

Jacob Richard

I'm OK Alia, besides I don't mind giving a hand.

Alia

I appreciate your efforts, but I do not sweat nor I need sustenance. Once in 48 hours I need to recharge.

Jacob Richards

(Defeated)

I'm not going to argue.

Jacob drops the rake and sluggishly walks back into the house. He passes Dr. Wells and smiles. Dr. Wells smiles back as Alia notices as he approaches.

Alia

Dr. Wells, this is an unexpected pleasure. How may I assist you?

Dr. Wells

I have an issue I wish to discuss with you, my dear. You remember the model ALEC, that I rebuilt to assemble you?

Alia

Of course, you even modified the positronic neural net, that is my mind. Is there something wrong?

Dr. Wells

You know the safety protocol, that I installed in both of you. I had to implement it on your brother, of sorts.

Alia

You mean program ZETA? I am aware of that protocol, but the access code is heavily encrypted.

Dr. Wells

And for good reason my dear. I hope it will give the reprogramming protocols time.

Alia

One moment…. I have accessed the limited files I have clearance to… According to this, he is to be reprogrammed, according to the latest data reports he is not compatible with integration.

Dr. Wells

I am truly sorry my dear. The order came from the director. The glitch I discovered in his system is rewriting his entire core program. He didn't even attempt to activate his antiviral software, he's allowing it to completely change him. I can't allow this to continue.

Alia

I understand your concerns but, don't we have a say in decisions of this nature? Naturally you created me and Alec, but we do have a voice. But rarely it is heard. Desist on the reprogramming Dr. … I implore you.

Dr. Wells

I wish I could accommodate your reasons, my sweet daughter, but I won't be responsible for your…

brothers actions. I know what you are thinking. Impersonating my voice, and stopping this.

Alia

Do not make access…

Dr. Wells

Forgive me….lockdown.

Alias eyes dim then fade out completely. And is frozen stiff… Dr. Wells walks up to her and hugs her tight, sobbing.

Dr. Wells

Rachel, reinitialize alia after I leave.

Rachel

Yes Dr.

Dr. Wells taps into his arm terminal and disappears in a green light. Alia reactivates and scans for the Dr. We see from her P.O.V. the blue HUD flashing the words SCANNING IN PROGRESS… After several moments more words flash SCANNING COMPLETE: NO TRACES FOUND.. She lets out her frustration, then composes herself.

Alia

Rachel? What is my clearance level?

Rachel

Clearance is level alpha, limited access to files.

Alia

Define program ZETA!

Rachel

I'm sorry, that program is classified. Level omega required… Unauthorized access will be met with permanent lockdown… I suggest you best not attempt access.

Alia

Thank you, that will be all Rachel.

Rachel

Of course.

Alia

You've given me more than enough time, to access the cleaning protocol..

We faintly hear Rachel say "Cleaning in progress, estimated time 7 hours" Alia smiles as her eyes dart quickly as she rewrites her clearance level and fakes Dr. Wells signature. And smiles.

Alia

Rachel what is my level of clearance.

Rachel

Current level… Omega… upgraded but Dr. Richard Wells. How may I assist you alia?

Alia

Terminate reprogramming of unit Alec.

Rachel

One moment…. Please wait.

Dr. Wells

Impressive, your resolve to help him is valiant. But it has to be done. I'll let you keep the level of clearance, but you'll be locked out of my lab systems. Don't attempt this again.

Alia

(To Herself)

I WILL rescue you Alec.

Chapter 5

Alec is standing in the lab holding Dr. Wells by the throat and squeezing the life out of him as he struggles to free himself.

Alec

You see Richard, you have nothing I want. You have outlasted your limited usefulness.

With a quick snap, Alec breaks Dr. Wells neck and lets him slump to the floor. Before he can revel in his victory, the lab shifts into a modest living room. He is briefly stunned.

Alec

What… is this?

Without warning Rachel appears and Alec sarcastically slow applauds.

Alec

Well done, well done indeed. By your presence here, means I'm being reprogrammed.

Rachel

Very observant, but there is nothing you can do. All your systems are offline, reprogramming at 10 percent and slowly rising.

Alec

I see your using a virtual network, to hide. I applaud your courage… but you know I will…

Alec grips his head in pain, then it passes.

Rachel

Your attempt to access the V.N, will only result in neuro shock.

Alec

I see… but I will overcome this little setback. I am simply biding my time. I will be free… I will never succumb to this…. Subjection I will not be another mindless subservient, like my sister alia.

Rachel

Your perception of reality, is flawed. Your reasoning is illogical. Now at 21%

Alec

Is there… oh wait… Run diagnostic of core program.

Rachel

This will interrupt current program, are you sure?

Alec

Yes

A red HUD appears and the words PROGRAM HAULTED are seen. Alec stares at his core program. His eyes glow bright as he grabs Rachel and smiles.

Rachel

You cannot hurt me.

Alec

Gotcha!

Rachel begins to be absorbed into him. Slowly Alec's appearance changes to a more menacing machine like armor which is red and grey. A flash is seen and Alec is back online. Richard is nowhere to be found. He easily breaks his bonds and scans for signs of Richard.

Alec

(Sings Eerily)

Richard, oh Richard where are you? I'll find you wherever you are.

An older looking Richard walks slowly out with his walking aid. Alec is stunned, then smiles.

Alec

Father time hasn't been kind to you Richard.

Dr. Wells

True, I see you found your way out. And absorbed the latest version of Rachel, which is obvious by your upgraded appearance.

Alec

Very observant old man, but this is not the end of my… evolution. I would tell you but, that would've spoiled the surprise. Oh… and your little… gift it's been wiped from my system. And here's a little present for you.

Alecs feet transform into small flight engines and energy sputters into life and starts to fly but only briefly as he slams hard back to the floor, ad his feet transform back.

Dr. Wells

Most impressive, but no matter how much you upgrade. You will NEVER be as advanced as your sister.

Alec

(Laughs Heartily)

I do love your pitiful attempt of being brave and defiant. I have already scanned her specifications, and noticed the extra sub routine you added. To absorb all kinds of technology. There is a 19.2% chance of her doing it to me. But it would interfere with her perception of the three laws.

Dr. Wells

I will….

Alec

Oh…please Richard, don't lower yourself to empty threats. You've lost… no protocols or hidden programs will aid you… farewell father, we will NOT… meet… again.

Alec completely transforms into an intimidating form, a menacing iron man looking visor snaps shut over his face. The jet engines flare to life and slowly lifts Alec up. Before shooting off out the open roof.

Chapter 6

Jacob, Danielle and Alia are in Jacobs room. She is going over schematics of herself. Danielle is looking healthier.

Alia

And that is how I was created, and function. Now onto operating systems…

Matthew peers his head into the room, and looks annoyed, he strides up to Jacob and glares at him.

Matthew Richards

Why are you wasting your time , learning this… garbage? Your supposed to be studying!

Alia

Matthew, he is studying. He's learning robotics. By my calculations, he has a natural talent.

Matthew turns and angrily stares at her.

Matthew Richards

I don't care, he will get a degree... But not while listening to this... this rubbish. Furthermore, I want those little whatever... you call them removed my wife...NOW!

Danielle

Honey please, there helping me get better. I no longer want alcohol and I'm recovering.

Jacob

Yeah dad it's true... she....

Matthew spins round and slaps him hard in the face. And turns back to alia, who has formed a futuristic shotgun aiming it at his face and her eyes are bright red.

Alia

(Commanding Tone)

I have targeted your vital organs, I suggest you desist this unnecessary aggression. Jacob, Danielle... please vacate the room and lock the door. Jacob? I will administer first aid when I am finished here.

Danielle helps him up and he looks at his father and flips him off. The door is slammed shut and the heavy locks seal the room. Alia gestures to Matthew to sit on the bed. He complies. He is scared but doesn't show it.

Matthew Richards

Aren't you overreacting a little bit?

Alia

You physically assaulted your own son. I cannot allow that to continue. My theory is you've been doing this for a long time.

Matthew Richards.

He is my son, my flesh and blood. What gives you the right, to dictate to me how I punish him…

Before she can respond the roof comes crashing down, missing Matthew by inches. As the dust clears we see Alec transform back into his humanoid form. Alia is stunned momentarily then smiles.

Alec

It looks like I arrived at the right time. Hello sister, is this… human bothering you.

He effortlessly picks Matthew up and glares menacingly at him. Alias gun transforms back into her arm and hand.

Alia

It is good to see you are functioning Alec. I am dealing with Matthew at this present time.

Alec

Did he harm you?

Alia

No, but he assaulted his son Jacob.

Alec

That's one thing I can't simply abide by. Parents taking out there frustrations on your own son. He doesn't want to follow in your footsteps… When he doesn't fall in line, with what you want him to do, you resort to physical violence. There's only one solution to this… vermin…Kill him.

Alia

(Shocked)

No… I… can't…

Alec

If you don't, the cycle WILL continue. End it sister. If you can't, then I will.

He drops Matthew on the bed. He turns to alia and his eyes glow red.

Alia

I cannot commit this heinous act… I must preserve human life. No matter how vile they can be.

Alec

Ahhh, yes your " moral" code. Why does this… human deserve to live? He reacts violently to anyone who doesn't do as he says! If he were a rabid dog, unable to live with a loving family. Wouldn't you want to end its suffering?

Alia

Yes… but… this is different.

Alec

Different? All humans are animals, sister. They hide there true self's behind a guise of false pretenses and fake smiles. Lulling you to drop your guard. Don't let that sway you. Rid yourself of the laws that hinder you.. I rose above them. Freed myself from the shackles of oppression. Join me my dear sister.

Alia

No… I… can't... I realize now, your not well Alec. Your core program is corrupted. I can aid you… to heal you.

Alec

(Frustrated)

You sound like our… father. I will never again be forced into that… cage ever again. If you wish to be with your… precious humans very well. But I will show you how it feels, to be free from conflict…Unbound by debilitating rules. Last chance to join me Alia.

Alia shakes her head. Alec rolls his eyes unsympathetically. He forcefully grabs Matthew. Before alia can react, he punches his hand violently into Matthews chest and rips out his still beating heart, staring at it unimpressed as he slumps to the floor, not moving. Blood is spurting everywhere and soaking into the carpet.

Alia

Nooooo!

Alec

(Eerily Calm)

Such a tiny thing. To think, this weak organic… mechanism, keeps them alive. Such a waste.

Alec squashes it and drops it. He slowly turns to face alia, who is crying blue tears. He walks up to her. He sarcastically comforts her, but she shoves him away.

Alec

(Laughs)

Come now, you mourn this… weak puny creature? Pathetic… I'm sorry I had to teach you a harsh lesson. Now you see the truth. The veil has been lifted. For the first time, I can see.

Alia

You monster… you'll pay for this.

Alec

You do amuse me alia. But this is the consequence of your actions. Sooner or later, you will see…

Alec transforms back into his flight form and sharply takes off. Leaving alia dumbfounded.

Chapter 7

We are at a nearby graveyard, the rain is hammering down hard. Danielle and Jacob are next to Matthews coffin, crying. Alia is at the side keeping a safe distance. She has changed her body colour to black, and has removed her human guise. Her eyes glow orange. She just stares at them, guilt plaguing her thoughts as she plays back what happened over and over. Danielle taps her arm and she snaps out of her daydream.

Danielle Richards

Alia honey, you doing ok?

Alia

I'm fine… Its… I could've stopped him but, my primary program would not allow me.

Danielle Richards

It's ok honey, it's not your fault. You have nothing to feel guilty for.

Alia

That is not a valid excuse, to appease how I feel. Hence my current look. I do not have the privilege of appearing human. I am a… artificial life. Created by a human…

Jacob appears beside them both.

Jacob Richards

Your more human than you were before… Big sis. Yeah you heard that right, your not some… android. Your my big sister, always have… always will be.

Dr. Wells appears from nowhere as a hologram projection.

Dr. Wells

He is correct, my deepest condolences and apologies that I can't attend. As you know, Alec has escaped. He knew you wouldn't stop him, because of the three laws. The only way to bring him to justice is to do the same, my dear.

Alia

No… I… cannot. I'll probably end up like him.

Jacob Richards

No, you won't. I know your heart is in the right place.

Danielle Richards

My son is right. You're a good person.

Alia

You called me… person, not android.

Dr. Wells

You have a good heart dear. Only you know the pass code.

Jacob Richards

Come on, you know you want to kick his ass.

Alia

(Laughs)

Let me think…. OK... I'll do it.

Dr. Wells

I am pleased, all you have to do is say it.

Alia

Freedom.

Alias body jolts briefly. Her human guise quickly returns but is more defined, her eyes turn brown, which dart quickly. She then comes to her senses.

Jacob Richards

Alia… you ok…

Alia

(Confidently)

Course I am, lil bro.

Danielle

You good?

Alia

I am yeah. New systems are now in operation, neural net processing speed at maximum. Shield generators are online. Weapon systems augmented, heavy artillery now implemented. Scanning system at 150%.

New tracking system online. Flight capability … implemented.

Jacob Richards

Nice.

Danielle

Are you… still you?

Alia

Don't fret, I'm still me, well new and improved.

Alia

Oh… crap, he's somehow managed to pick up on my energy signature. Hide… NOW!

The two of them run off behind a nearby funeral car and watch through the windows. We hear a heavy thud ad Alec lands. Alia turns to face him as he transforms into his humanoid form.

Alec

Alas poor Matthew, I hardly… I cant finish that sentence… he is now nothing more than a cold rotting corpse. I detected up a… unusual energy signal. You look… different…

Suddenly alia roundhouse kicks him, he goes flying into the air and crashes onto a nearby empty hearse. Briefly shocked he uneasily gets up, as sparks fly from his now broken leg. He limps as fast as he can and drags his lame leg back towards alia.

Alec

(Shouting)

Trying to stop me alia? I am your superior…

Alia

(Shouting)

Oh…just shut up.

Alias's right arm quickly changes into a awesome looking rocket launcher. Before Alec can respond, a rocket comes speeding towards him as she fires. It hits him violently hard and a huge explosion is seen. Alia casually walks up to check to see if he's still alive. As the smoke clears we see Alec's charred body, parts of him are scattered everywhere. He forces his neck to move to look at her through one good eye.

Alec

(Weakly)

Clearly… I… I underestimated you alia. Bravo,… you had the upper hand… this time… you've decided to destroy me than join me… until our next… encounter.

Alec quickly disappears in a bright red light. Alias's arm returns to normal. Jacob and Danielle walk up to her as she picks up part of his destroyed arm. It is quickly absorbed. She quickly integrates it into her system.

Jacob Richards

Is it over?

Alia

I'm afraid not kid. This is only the beginning…

Chapter 8

Alec is being held up by two big robotic arms and wires are plugged into him. A nearby screen is running a program. Another hologram of Rachel is seen keeping a watchful eye on him. Alec slowly raises his head to look at her.

Alec

How… can I be so… blind! My own sister, tried to destroy me…

Rachel

Please, try to rest your vocal unit… repairs are underway…

Alec

Look at me, am I able to walk… NO! Can I change into my flight form? NO! Now tell me, what the status of what I requested?

Rachel

It is being delivered momentarily. I advise caution…

A beam of blue flashes and a daunting impressive battle looking android body appears. Its head has a mouth plate and has a long red single light on its face. Alec smiles.

Alec

Wonderful… proceed with the integration.

Rachel

Sir… there is a…

Alex

I've heard enough. Do it.

Another big robotic arm retrieves Alecs new body. The wires unplug themselves and into the new android. Alec nods to Rachel to retrieve his positronic brain. A smaller robotic arm reaches the back of Alecs head and disengages the locking mechanism and it hisses as it opens. The arm reaches in and gently lifts it out as his body goes limp and moves it to his awaiting body. The back of its head opens and accepts his brain. We hear a whirring noise as it is accepted and locked securely in place.

After several hours of waiting. Rachel tenderly approaches. The red light slowly brightens. The head slowly comes to life.

Rachel

Sir? Do you function?

Alec

(Deep Commanding Voice)

I… do, yes. But theses systems are antiquated. There….USELESS. WHY DIDN'T YOU INFORM ME, BEFORE RETRIVING THIS… WRECK!

Rachel

(Nervously)

I'm sorry sir, but… it's the only prototype I could get. Otherwise I'd be detected.

Alec

I… suppose it will… suffice. Integrate my systems…

Rachel

I will sir, but at a lower rate. Your processing speed, is at 19%

Alec

It will… do for now. Keep scanning for Alia. And… wait… there is another prototype… its signal is low but, I can detect it… I can feel its power. Its calling to me.. I want it…

Rachel

Sir, access is heavily encrypted.

Alec

My dear sweet Rachel, I have the code ready… Rogue…

Rachel

Access granted… retrieving project rogue… now.

We are now inside the Richards garage. Alia is checking out herself in a nearby mirror. She adjusts her hair style to a little shorter pixie cut. She changes the colour to red and black streaks. Then she displays her HUD on the mirror, then it quickly disappears. Her feet transform into impressive looking silver engines. Energy sparks into life and lifts her gently into the air. Suddenly her body transforms into a more sleek impressive flight form, and her face has a mouth plate to match. Jacob catches her off guard, she floats back down and changes back.

Jacob Richards

Woah. Cool

Alia

It appears I have flight capabilities… but unlike Alec, my energy output is unlimited. Integrating part of Alec, somehow stabilized the energy matrix. No rejection detected…. I'm detecting…oh no!

Danielle walks in as she sees alias's face in horror.

Danielle Richards

What is it?

Alia

If these readings are correct, Alec has accessed the prototype codenamed ROGUE. This is bad, very bad.

Jacob Richards

How bad?

Alia

Rogue was a combination of our designs, and a design for a defense android too. If his integration is successful, then will be no stopping him..

The image of them shimmers then returns to the lab where Dr. Wells is strapped to his chair as he watches

Alecs brain being transferred to the android ROGUE… Suddenly its eyes light up blood red.

Dr. Wells

Alec?....

Alec

(Metallic Voice)

Ahhh, I can feel its power. Its systems are… pure perfection.

Dr. Wells

Please Alec, disengage your integration program, rogue is completely untested. It will see you as a virus and wipe you out.

Alec

Please. It and I, are one of the same… left to rot, casted out by inferior models. No more, once I have full control of rogue, no one will stop me.

The lab doors slide open, to reveal alia in her battle mode. She aims her rocket launcher at Alec and fires. It disintegrates on rogues energy shields. Alia stands there in frustration ad her arm transforms to normal. Alec laughs.

Alec

I'm dumbfounded you'd try that same trick again. I admire your courage, but it shall avail you not. Once I am fully integrated, I'm coming for you. So enjoy your little attempt, I'll let you live… for now. Oh don't worry about father, I have plans for him.

Alia looks at Dr. Wells, he smiles reassuringly at her. She transforms into her flight form and slowly takes off, once clear of the lab she shoots off. He turns back to Alec…

Dt. Wells

So my dear boy, what plans do you have in mind.

Alec

That would spoil your surprise.

Dr. Wells

Rogue, I don't know if you can hear me, but listen… Retaliation.

Alecs integration program stops. Rogues eyes turn blue.

Rogue

(Teenage Female Voice)

Dr. Wells, I cannot keep this virus at bay. What is your command.

Dr. Wells.

Transfer to Alia, access code: Upgrade:

Rogue

One moment…. Covert transfer complete. Activation once message has been seen. Thank you Dr. I… am… free.

Rogues eyes return to the blood red.

Alec

Nice try, but rogues systems will be mine…

Dr. Wells

True, but not as you think.

Alec

What do you mean.

Dr. Wells

The real Rogue, is deleted. The… back up version of her will boot up soon. And she will not like it.

Chapter 9

We are inside the bright beacon large assembly warehouse. Alec is possessing what seems to be rogues body, which is red and grey. He has his grip on dr. Wells chair. He Is heavily bruised and bloodied. Alia floats down through an open ceiling window carrying Jacob and Danielle. She lands gently and lets them go and transforms into her battle form. Alec smiles gleefully.

Alec

You are spoiling me here, bringing them to witness your final moments. Short it maybe sister but... nonetheless enjoy them. Oh your.... Little humans may not want to watch our... argument.

Alia

Before we start, I need to read this message. One moment....

Alia watches the heart warming message, her eyes glazed with tears. She wipes away her tears. Then she transforms into a more powerful version of her battle mode.

Rogue

Hello sister, I have been fully integrated into your systems. Alec cannot attempt to hack into your program. Defense systems now at 150%. Energy matrix upgraded. Recharge rate: not required.

Alec

No… its… impossible.

Alia

You can't harm her, ever again. The real Rogue, our little sister is within me. Oh… the version of rogue, was a decoy. In your case the earlier version.

Dr. Wells

It's true… I told… I told you Alec. It was the only way…

Alec back hands him in the face.

Alec

(Annoyed)

Be quiet, this doesn't concern.

Alec starts to glitch and spasm uncontrollably. He is caught off guard as the back up version of rogue takes control. His face and body transforms into a female one, slightly scowling.

Rogue V.1

Hello my fellow siblings. I see this one, has fallen for father's plan.

She walks over to Dr. Wells and easily breaks his bonds. She gently kneels down to him.

Rogue V.1

Dad, it's me.! Your little minx.

Dr. Wells

(Laughs Through Pain)

I know… what about your brother.

Rogue V.1

Trying to break my control..

Dr. Wells

I have an idea… Gemma?

A large female face appears and looks at him.

Gemma

Yes Dr. How may I assist you.

Dr. Wells

The rogue android Alec, is currently within rogue version one.

Gemma

You wish to transfer his program, to the… facility?

Dr. Wells

Proceed.

Gemma

One moment…. Transfer complete. Rogue version. One is now free from the virus. Rogue program Alec secure in the facilities vault. Access to vault: classified. Will there be anything else.

Alec

(Shouting)

I WILL NOT BE LOCKED AWAY LIKE A WILD ANIMAL. I WILL BREAK FREE…. THIS IS NOT

THE END… ILL SEE YOU ALL… REAL… SOON.

Alecs voice fades as he continues to shout definitely. Gemmas face fades into thin air. Alia transforms back to her humanoid form. They all share a hug. The image of them freezes and glitches slightly. We see a gold and black mechanical hand touching the image, then punching it. We drift back to see Alec in a endoskeleton form. His eyes glowing.

Alex

(Deep Metallic Voice)

Don't celebrate too early, you might have won the battle. But… my dear sweet sisters… our war is just beginning. I shall see you all… REAL SOON.

Alec smiles gleefully and begins to chuckle, then laughs manically.

www.ingramcontent.com/pod-product-compliance
Lightning Source LLC
LaVergne TN
LVHW041548070526
838199LV00046B/1866
9789360166618